Maya's Treasure

Laurie Smollett Kutscera

P Peter Pauper Press, Inc.
WHITE PLAINS, NEW YORK

Published by Peter Pauper Press, Inc.
202 Mamaroneck Avenue
White Plains, New York 10601 USA

Library of Congress Cataloging-in-Publication Data

Names: Kutscera, Laurie Smollett, author, illustrator.
Title: Maya's treasure / Laurie Smollett Kutscera.
Description: First edition. | White Plains, New York : Peter Pauper Press,
2021. | Audience: Ages 3-8 | Audience: Grades K-1 | Summary: Each
morning Maya and her sister collect seashells, scrub them to a sparkle,
and string them together, but when Alita throws away shells she deems too ugly,
Maya, remembering words of her grandmother, turns the clunky
shells into a helpful and beautiful wind chime.
Identifiers: LCCN 2021015734 | ISBN 9781441337627 (hardcover)
Subjects: CYAC: Shells--Fiction. | Sisters--Fiction. |
Individuality--Fiction. | Creative ability--Fiction.
Classification: LCC PZ7.1.K894 May 2021 | DDC [E]--dc23
LC record available at https://lccn.loc.gov/2021015734

ISBN 978-1-4413-3762-7

Manufactured for Peter Pauper Press, Inc.
Printed in China

7 6 5 4 3 2 1

Visit us at www.peterpauper.com

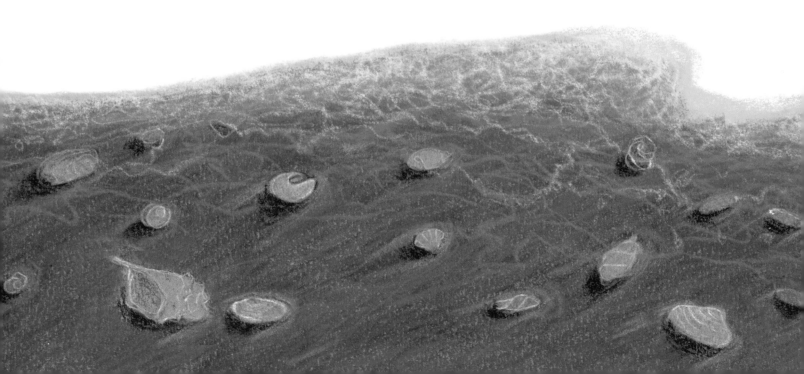

For Enid,
who found the magic in everything.

Maya and Alita lived by the sea,
where the tide rippled silver,
and the ocean floor offered its treasures
by the light of the waning moon.

Each morning, when the sun rose,
the sisters collected the gifts the surf
had left behind.

Tiny glistening shells, bleached and scalloped,
curvy conch shells where hermit crabs had once found refuge.

Maya and Alita scooped them up.
Scrubbing, drying, and polishing them
until they sparkled like stars.

Early on, Grandmother taught them the family tradition
of making shell jewelry.

"Even the tiniest nub can be quite beautiful," she'd whisper
as she threaded them, one by one.

"You just have to find the magic in it."

As Maya grew, Grandmother's words still echoed softly in her ears. Her legacy lived on in earrings, bracelets, and amulets.

"This will make a pretty hairpiece," Maya said.

"And these, a lovely bracelet," Alita replied.

Alita dropped a few shells into her basket,
then tossed the rest back into the sand.

"What's wrong with those?" Maya asked.

"Those are ugly. No one will ever buy them!"

Maya disagreed.

She picked up the shells her
sister had discarded, cracked
and marred in the last storm.
As she turned them over,
Grandmother's words filled
her heart.

"... just find the magic."

Each day, Maya quietly gathered the ugly shells her sister had thrown back,
determined to make something beautiful out of them.
But all that came was …

a clunky bracelet,

heavy earrings,

and a mismatched necklace.

Nothing seemed to work.

Maya raised the odd-looking necklace and sighed. Maybe Alita was right. *"Why would anyone want this?"* she thought.

She had just about given up hope when *WHOOSH!* A breeze pushed through and shook the palms. That's when an idea struck!

Maya strung the shells with knotted strands of hemp, then tied them to a thick piece of driftwood.

When she finished, she held her creation up to the wind.

"What is that sound?" her sister asked.

"They're chimes!" Maya beamed.

"You used those dreadful shells? No one will ever buy them!"

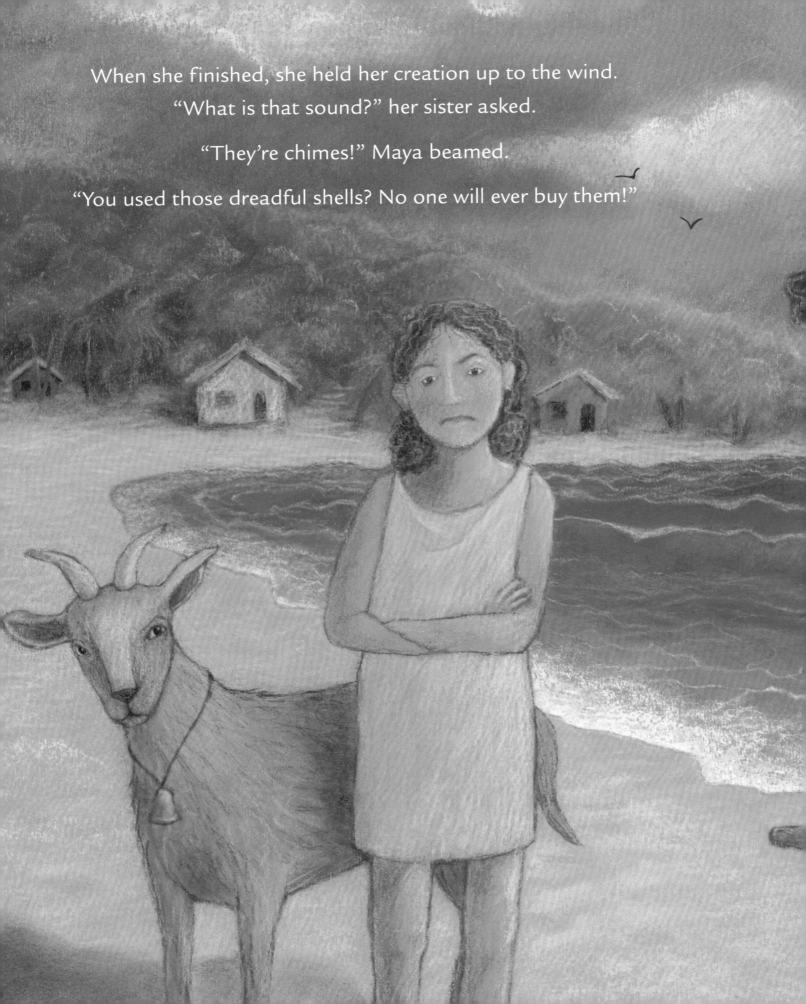

But Maya didn't care. She loved how their weathered shapes shifted and glimmered in the early evening light.

That night, Maya hung the chimes from a branch outside her window. When their soothing sound rang out in the breeze, she dreamt of her grandmother and remembered how they danced in the moonlight.

She and her grandmother twirled and spun while
the sound of the chimes grew loud—louder still until
they rattled and clanged like a ship's bell.

Maya jumped up from her pillow.

She woke her sister, and together they hurried through the village,
warning the townspeople that a storm drew near.

The wind whipped and snapped while villagers rushed to higher ground, far from the surging sea.

"How did you know a storm was brewing?" they asked.
"We heard nothing!"

Alita pointed to her sister's handiwork, clanging wildly from the tree below.
"Maya's chimes warned us!" she exclaimed.

"How remarkable they are!" the villagers agreed.
"And sturdy to stand up to such fierce winds!"
Maya clutched her necklace and smiled.

Soon enough, Maya's chimes rang throughout the village.

They clattered their warning when the wind howled.
They clinked and clanked when the seas churned.

And on balmy evenings,
they chimed softly,
when the tide rippled silver,
and the ocean floor offered its treasures
by the light of the waning moon.